Also by Conley Stone McAnally

Tales From Homer

Tales From the Lake

Wilson Bay: Tales From an Eskimo Village

Jump, Alaska: Tales From the Interior

O'Brian's Black & Tan: Tales From an Irish Pub

Ashwood: Tales From the Porch

Pantano Wash

The McShanes: Reluctant Warriors

Four From Fillmore

Available from Amazon
or www.pharaohpublishingusa.com

The Village Archeology Saga Continues...

The
Portland
Express

By Conley Stone McAnally

PHARAOH PUBLISHING USA

THE PORTLAND EXPRESS

By Conley Stone McAnally

Managing Editor: Richard Andrews

PHA023 • ISBN 978-0692713969

Pharaoh Publishing USA
www.pharaohpublishingusa.com

Cover art used under license

Produced and designed by Seann McAnally

For Uncle Frank
Who lost a leg on the rails
and
Abraham Lincoln McAnally
who caused a train wreck.

It's a long story. Don't ask.

Contents

Preface

The first time I was on a train was when I was a Cub Scout. The Cub Master decided that the Pack ought to take a ride on a train because he felt like passenger rail service was going to be a thing of the past by the time we Cubs were grown. He saw the construction of the Interstate Highway system and the increase of passenger plane service as being the wave of the future and rail service would only be used to haul freight, with an occasional hobo hopping aboard. He was almost right but he failed to see the creation of Amtrak and government subsidies.

Being a World War II veteran he had no fear in loading twenty-five nine to eleven year-old boys on a local commuter train for a day's journey to a town east of us, eating lunch in the dining car and returning later that evening.

I really don't remember much about the trip except the food that was served on the train – beef and noodles –was very tasty. I am sure my tiny band of brothers behaved as well as any Cub Scouts ever did on such an excursion, and it was only coincidental that our adult leader suffered some sort of nervous disorder and resigned as Cub Master soon afterwards.

The next time I rode a train was at the behest and direction of Professor Simpson, Dean of the University Village Archeology Department. I, as Special Project Officer for the department, reported directly to Professor Simpson - my boss, nemesis, and most ardent critic of my style, demeanor, and methodology. The fact that the last three projects he had given me turned out to be a publicity and financial bonanza for the University strained our relationship. You'd think it would work just the opposite. University politics is something that I have failed to understand, let alone master; and trying to comprehend the academic ego hurts my brain. Besides, I think when it is all said and done, Professor Simpson just does not like my fedora.

It is always a long way to one's boss' office when summoned by his secretary. You have a lot of time to go over your past behavior to see which inadvertent slip of the tongue or article you once wrote that someone is just now taking offense at and decided to tattle or at least make sure your boss knew of the displeasure. Having been kicked out of an Eskimo village for such a thing once left me a little leery. I never really believed that the pen is mightier than the sword but I always thought it was at least a close cousin.

As I entered Dean Simpson's office he peered at me over his spectacles and waved for me to sit opposite him in a chair whose legs had been made shorter than his throne. It was the type of trick someone like Donald Trump would use to insure you knew who was in charge.

"Mr. McAnally, I assume you have heard of the Portland Express?"

"No, sir I have not."

"Well, I don't know why you should have," he said disgustedly. "The Portland Express is only the first railroad to serve the north part of North America and connects Portland, Maine, and Portland, Oregon, and more small towns in between than any other railroad in history. It's been around for 100 years and is celebrating the bicentennial of the birth of its founder, Stanly Hoginfessor, next month. The upcoming event has received a lot of national media coverage and the CEO, Stanly Hoginfessor III, was featured on the cover of Time Magazine last week. Why should you have heard about it?" His sarcasm was syrupy thick and did not escape me.

I thought that his comments were rather cold and insensitive and downright rude. How did he know that I didn't have time to pay attention to world events because I was taking care of an old maid aunt at a convent that did not allow secular news to interfere with prayers, meditation, and reflection? I hadn't, of course, but how did he know? "Well, on second thought it does sort of ring a bell," I said, trying to regroup and maintain some sort of professional dignity and lose my deer-in-the-headlights look.

"No matter," he responded, "they have heard of you and your knack of taking a very simple assignment and making a big deal out of it."

I assumed he was talking about my last three books that the University Press had published and made required reading, thus requiring purchase, for all students in the Village Archeology Department. They were selling pretty well among alumni, too.

The University made a nice chunk of change from the sales, whereas I received no royalties at all. I had been informed by the University lawyers that since I was under assignment and employed by the school when the books were written I had no legal right to financial compensation. They had me sign a paper stating that I agreed and at the same time offered me a contract as a tenured special project officer for the Village Archeology Department. What can I say; a job is a job, and the money ain't bad.

Professor Simpson told me that the Portland Express, on its next run between the two Ports – as the company execs called it – requested that I ride the train the entire route and interview people along the way so they could get a better handle on what type of person rode the train instead of taking a plane, automobile, or bus.

My specific task was to select people at random, engage them in conversation and see if there was a common thread among them. I assumed - and was proven correct later on - the information I acquired would be used by the railroad's marketing department to help pinpoint direct advertising.

It sounded like a pretty easy assignment but I had to ask, "What does that have to do with Village Archeology, Doctor Simpson?"

He rubbed his brow slowly in despair, like he was explaining something to a first year grad student for the fourth time and who should have known better than to ask such a stupid question in the first place. "Village Archeology is more than just things in the dirt, or manuscripts left in vacant buildings, or stories told from a porch. It is about people. It is about the emotions people have. Call it emotional archeology if you wish. It is all part of the same human experience. You need to dig into the heart of the people you meet as well as the dirt they stand upon. Then you will be in a position to discover why people do what they do and what brings them to a given place at a given time. You need to search for the common denominator. Reconstruct the steps that created the society and culture we now inhabit. And besides, they are paying the University for your time and research results. Your train leaves tomorrow evening from the local Amtrak station and will take you to Portland, Maine. Have a good trip Mr. McAnally. Do you have any questions or have anything to say?"

I had several questions and a comment or two but thought I would just leave them in my head. I did have a strange desire to yell out "all aboard" but didn't think it would be appropriate under the circumstances.

I

Abraham Lincoln Julian

"All aboard!" The cry from track 23 west bound seemed appropriate enough given the circumstances. Mr. Julian, the conductor, would not let me yell out the words, and he was very adamant. "Everyone has a job to do on this train, and making sure everyone is on board in a safe and timely manner is mine. See what I mean, young fellow?"

Well, yes, I did see what he meant. The International Brotherhood of the United Conductors' Union wanted to protect their positions from those of us who thought the job looked pretty easy. I had no idea of what kind of apprenticeship was involved but was sure they wanted to keep it a secret. Seems like most anything with the name of brotherhood in the title is guarded from those who can not produce a secret word, a handshake that challenges ones dexterity, or a union card.

Mr. Julian was a very impressive looking individual along with his baritone voice, tailor-made blue suit, white starched collar, and black string bowtie - all of which accented his ebony skin. He would be my first interview, I decided. But given the fact that he was such a busy man, my interview had to be snatched in bits and pieces. It was obvious why Mr. Julian was on the train so my enquiry centered on why and how he went to work for The Portland Express.

Abraham Lincoln Julian was born to Martha and George Julian, who owned a farm and apple orchid near Rainsville, Ohio. The family grew just enough vegetables to sustain them year round. Selling apples and their by-products – cider, jelly, preserves – to the local restaurants took care of the cash flow.

Abe, as Mr. Julian was called by friends and family, was just thirteen when he convinced his father to try to sell some items down at the train station. It turned out to be a good idea because by the time Abe was fifteen, the family had increased their commodities to honey and mini apple pies that were sold directly to the train company to serve in its dining cars.

Abe became acquainted with the dining car manager that everyone just called Chef. He was very impressed by Chef. It was not common in

Rainsville to see another Negro other than his family members and especially one who was in charge of something.

One day Abe entered the kitchen car and found no one there except Chef. Chef was drinking a cup of coffee and saw the puzzled expression on Abe's face. As if Chef knew what Abe was thinking, Chef said, "We have a three hour layover and I let the crew go into town for a bit. Sit and have a cup of coffee with me; better yet, are those apple biscuits you got there? If so let's have a buckles." Abe had no idea what buckles were or was, but what he was carrying were apple biscuits.

Chef placed a saucer in front of each of them, placed a biscuit on each saucer, cut the biscuits in half and poured coffee over each. He then sprinkled them with sugar. "This is a poor man's dessert," Chef said; "you can't buy this in any restaurant. Your honey tastes good on them also. Remember, they are Buckles not Buckle."

The Buckles was good and the next Buckles was just as good. Before you knew it, Chef and Abe had eaten all of the apple biscuits Abe had.   So much for the family profits this trip, Abe thought. However, Chef bought enough apples and jars of jelly to make up for the loss.

From then on Abe and Chef became very good

friends--well, as much as a 50 plus year-old man and a fifteen plus year-old boy could be under the circumstances. One day Abe went into the kitchen car with enough biscuits for all the cooks and dishwashers and announced that it was his birthday. He was sixteen and wanted to share in his grand announcement with those who had become his good friends.

"Gentlemen, and you too, Chef," began Abe, as everyone laughed, "I have decided that I am going to put in my application with the Portland Express to train to be a chef just like you Chef. I have talked it over with mom and dad and they have agreed it was about time for me to move on. My younger brothers and sisters can help run the farm orchard and sales now. I have trained them well." Everyone cheered, that is everyone except Chef. Chef asked Abe if he would like to go to the empty dining car and have a Buckles.

Abe told Chef he was going to talk to him first but, "I just sort of got caught up in the moment. I would like to work here with you, be your assistant or something like that."

"Well, perhaps; let me talk to the conductor about the matter."

The next week Abraham was told by Chef that he had talked to the head conductor who said there was an opening coming up very soon and Abe could start on the next trip through Rainsville. But Abe would serve as an assistant porter in the sleeping car section of the train, not in the food preparation area.

"I thought I would be working with you here in the kitchen," replied a disappointed Abe.

"Look, son, you have more talent than is necessary to be a train chef. It is a dead end job, and I isn't that old so you won't be taking my spot soon. As a porter you will be on a track, no pun intended, to be a conductor, a passenger train car conductor, eventually. Then you will be my boss some day." With that said, Chef gave Abe a sleeping car porter uniform, and Abe thought it was the most beautiful white coat, black hat, and string bowtie he had ever seen. "I want you to get off on the right foot. You got to look sharp when you are dealing with train passengers. Make sure you are always polite."

Abe, now referred to only as Mr. Julian, had taken Chef's advice to heart, worked hard and became the youngest conductor and eventually chief conductor the Portland Express had ever employed. That was close to 50 years ago by the time he talked to me.

2

To Sea the World

We pulled out of the Portland Union Station as I was unpacking and storing my clothes and toiletries in the corner of a small sleeping facility it appeared I was to share with two other fellows. One was a cook in the dining car and the other was an assistant sleeping car porter.

The two men worked alternating twelve hour shifts and seldom talked to one another. I, in turn, spent most of my time combing the passenger cars looking for potential interviewees, eating in the dining car, and organizing my notes in the observation car. Now and then our paths would cross, or I should say we would bump into one another, literally, trying to shave, shower, or dress. Even if we had all been close friends it would have been awkward. Being strangers and thrown into such close proximity, it was an incentive for the three of us to not hang around the cubical when not sleeping.

The trip to Portland, Oregon was to take us five or maybe six days, depending on how much freight was scheduled from the Pacific Coast and Great Plains, "and who knows what else," said one of my compartment companions.

There were going to be plenty of stops for different reasons along the way, such as taking off trash, re-supplying food, fuel and drink, picking up and letting off passengers, and being sidetracked, which happened much more frequently than I would have imagined if I had bothered to imagine it at all. The whole train travel process was an education in and of itself. For instance, I had never understood the significance of the term 'sidetracked' until then. It was a small 'ah-ha' moment but one nonetheless. However, I digress.

As I was entering the dining car I noticed a young sailor sitting alone. I slipped into the seat across from him. He was more than eager to talk. His name was Donnie McGraw, "That's Seaman First Class Donnie McGraw," he said with some pride and authority.

Donnie had just finished advanced training at the Bush Naval Air Base. What kind of training he did not specify nor did he talk a whole lot about military matters during the entire trip. Loose lips still sink ships, and I expected nothing less from our men in uniform. But he was pretty talkative concerning other things.

He was from a small town in Montana, called Ulysses. When I looked like I had no idea where that was he said "not very far from Grant City." I still had no idea where that was either but I let it go.

Donnie joined the Navy to see the world. He had never ventured very far off the farm. He said he was taking the train to see the sights along the tracks. The Navy flew him to Chicago for his basic training at the Great Lakes Naval Base, and his trip was mostly at night so he had not seen much of the countryside. After basic they put him on a sailing ship all the way up the Saint Lawrence Seaway to the training facility.

"So why are you now taking the train?" I asked.

"To see what I should see before I go to sea," he said with a chuckle.

The farm where Donnie grew up was in the middle of nothing even by central western Montana standards. His first few years of schooling took place in a one room school house, and then he and what passed for neighborhood kids attended the Grant City Consolidated School District until they reached high school age. He and his eighth grade graduating class, all eight of them, then attended

Appomattox Senior High School, which had a combined total of 67 students and four years later he and eleven other of his classmates received their diplomas. Donnie ranked sixth in his graduating class.

Early one evening after a blistering day of bucking bales and fixing fence, the family was just sitting down to dinner when they heard a man's voice yell out, "Hello, anyone home?" The entire family, all three of them, was startled since few visitors ever came by and those who did always came round to the back door and just walked in.

Mr. McGraw answered the knock. There he found a young man in a naval uniform nervously grinning through the screen door.

The sailor introduced himself as Allen Smead. Lost, with his car broken down he asked "I wonder if you could tell me where the nearest garage is and if I could use your phone."

"Of course," said Mr. McGraw.

It would be a couple of hours before the tow truck arrived and Lt JG Allen Smead was asked if he was hungry and would like a bite of supper. He said yes and yes.

Allen Smead was a recruiting officer for the

United States Navy. He said he was combing the
area for recruits around the Grant County area but
somehow made a wrong turn, became disoriented
and then his vehicle broke down. "I'm lucky I broke
down close to your place."

It was Donnie's mother who broached the
subject. "You find anyone wanting to join the Navy
around here? Not much water is there? Do young
men really see the world while in the Navy and do
they really learn a trade they can use in civilian life?
How long does a young man have to join for? Do
you have to take a test? How long after a boy signs
up does he have to leave? Could a boy sign up now
and not leave until the fall harvest? Oh, Mr. Smead,
would you like another piece of cherry pie?"

Mrs. McGraw wanted the best for her son.
She had gone to Mountain View State College
in northeast Montana for two years before she
married Mr. McGraw and moved to the farm. She
did not regret it, but even though Donnie had only
graduated 6 out of a class of 12 she knew he had
more talent than was needed on the farm. College
was not affordable but learning a trade in the
military was, so everyone said. She felt like God
brought Allen Smead to their farm and it was His
will that Donnie become a sailor.

Mr. McGraw, if asked, would just as soon
Donnie stay on the farm, but he wasn't consulted

about the matter; and between Mrs. McGraw and the Naval Recruiter, Donnie signed on the dotted line. Mr. McGraw did say that there was no need to wait till the fall harvest. He could get by as long as Mrs. McGraw pitched in, so when the tow truck came to pick up Allen, Donnie went too. Two days later Donnie was sworn in as a raw recruit at the Great Lake's Naval Training Center. Six weeks later he got a weekend pass.

Donnie met a girl while on that pass. He showed me her picture. She was a striking looking girl and very provocative as she clung upside down on the pole. I asked him where he met her exactly and he said at a bar on State Street named Butcher's. "Don't get the wrong impression though, she is a nice girl.

"She is going to meet me when I get to Portland Naval Station in Oregon. Poor gal has been waiting for me all this time while I finished advanced training in Maine. I am supposed to report in to Oregon the first of next month after my week's leave at home in Ulysses. I wanted her to come with me to meet mom and dad, but she said she had to give notice at her work and dancers were hard to find. It's all arranged though. We checked into the cost of a plane ticket so I went ahead and wired her the money to buy one. I am supposed to call her as soon as I get to Portland so she will know when to buy the ticket."

I excused myself gracefully and without comment. I left to find another person to interview, wishing I was not a cynic.

3

Visiting Day

Our first major stop was in Bing Bang, Vermont. A few people got on the train but more seemed to be getting off, but without baggage of any kind.

We were there about an hour. Just as we were about to leave the station I noticed Donnie racing to re-board the train. I had not seen him get off. I wondered if it had anything to do with that lady friend of his.

I asked Mr. Julian about the oddity of the mass exodus of passengers at Bing Bang, and he told me that it was visiting day at the Bing Bang State Prison. He explained that the passengers had no luggage because they would not be spending the night in Bing Bang but would catch the east bound train back to wherever they came from.

One lady I had noticed was getting on the

train carrying plenty of baggage and as I was to find out later a lot more baggage that wasn't visible. I thought she might be someone interesting to interview. With the help of a cleaning steward and a five dollar bill I managed to be shown to a seat next to the lady.

Withy my effervescent personality and boyish grin I managed to find out the following: Her name was May Sue Lewis. She had just been fired as a security officer at the State Prison. It took me awhile to find out why she got fired, but eventually she let me know it was because she had become overly friendly with an inmate.

"He wasn't guilty of the crime he was convicted of; I know for a fact," she said. "It was a setup and the police just wanted to make an arrest and clear their books so they picked on Jessie and framed him. He never shot and killed anyone."

Jessie was serving forty years for second degree murder. She said that she met him about two years ago when he was attending an art class she was responsible for monitoring. "He painted such wonderful pictures, all of them had a religious theme, and some are even hanging in churches all over the eastern seaboard."

He began to have so many requests for his paintings that prison officials assigned her to handle the logistics of the requests, production, and distribution of the artwork. It was good publicity for the prison and made church patrons feel like they were doing something to stem crime by helping a poor soul find the path to righteousness and salvation. Unfortunately for Jessie, the parole board didn't look at things the same way. Jessie had been denied parole five times in the last twenty years.

Jessie and Mary Sue worked closely together and eventually the line was crossed. Crossing the line between inmate and soulmate never happens all at once. It just sort of happens: a nice word here, a small compliment there, a favor now and then, maybe a phone call; it takes many forms. Before one knows it, someone is in love and it is usually the soulmate who is supposed to be doing the guarding.

Mary Sue handled all Jessie's art distribution and apparently did it well enough that the administration did not have to get involved on a day to day basis. That suited them just fine - both of the thems. (Parole board and Mary and Jesse if I just confused you.) Mary Sue had a lot of latitude and license as to how she handled Jessie's affairs.

There was a small little church in Oak Dale, New York, not far down the line whose pastor wanted a picture of the Virgin Mary holding the baby Jesus – a pretty standard request. The

problem was that they wanted the picture in time
for Christmas which was not enough time for Jessie
to create one. Normally Jessie and Mary Sue would
just politely say no; it was impossible, but the cousin
of the president of the parole board was a deacon
of the church, and the parole board president had
promised that Jessie would paint them one in time
for the midnight candlelight service.

"Impossible," Jessie cried to Mary Sue.

"Well, perhaps not," Mary Sue mused.

Mary Sue went to the largest Catholic Church
in Bing Bang, where she knew a painting was
housed similar to the one the Oak Dale church had
requested. It was in the basement archives and
seldom visited by anyone, and she was sure that no
one other than she knew the painting even existed.
She had stumbled on it by accident while she was
doing research on religious compositions for Jessie.
It was easier to remove the painting from the church
and place in her van than she thought it would be
and easier still to get it inside the prison to Jessie's
art studio.

The plan was for Jessie to paint over the
painting with fresh paint, making it look newer
than it really was. It only took a couple of days and
Mary Sue was able to crate and send the work off
to its new home in Oak Dale in plenty of time for

Christmas. Jessie smelled freedom. Just one more task remained to cover up the deception.

Jessie started working on a picture just like the one he had sent to Oak Dale. He had a pretty could eye for composition and color and remembered most of the details except some facial features that were nondescript. Mary Sue sneaked the finished picture back into the basement archives of St. Andrews and all would have been well but two things happened simultaneously.

At the next meeting of the parole board, Jessie's name was submitted. Apparently the pastor had been pleased by the painting and his cousin, i.e., parole board president, decided that perhaps Jessie wasn't such a bad guy after all and convinced the rest of the board to take a closer look at Jessie. They hired a private investigator who was a retired Federal Marshal named Tim O'Sullivan and cousin to the governor.

At the same time, retired FBI agent Steven O'Sullivan, brother to Tim and thus related to the governor, was hired by the McGennis family to investigate allegations that the priest at St. Andrews had misappropriated church funds. The priest of course denied everything and welcomed an audit. One place that got audited was the basement archives at St. Andrews. Steven O'Sullivan took photographs and cataloged each item in the archives and did a complete forensic financial audit and found nothing out of line.

Brother Tim's background check for the parole board was uncomplicated because there was much less to analyze since Jessie's whereabouts had been pretty well established for the last twenty years and he had received glowing reports about his behavior from his case worker - Mary Sue Lewis.

It was a family tradition of the O'Sullivan clan to eat Sunday dinner at Papa and Mother O'Sullivan's house. While the children were playing lawn darts in the back yard and the women cleaned up after supper, the men would gather in the parlor and watch whatever seasonal sporting event was playing on television, argue politics, discuss last week's doings, or snooze. It was during one of these gatherings that Tim and Steven started trading stories about their latest jobs.

Steven happened to bring along the photographs of the items in the church archives. As Tim was rummaging though the pile he stopped on a particular picture studied it for awhile and asked Steven how long these pictures had been in the archives.

"Well, Father O'Malley says they have not seen the light of day for at least ten years, and only a few people even venture down in the basement. Why do you ask?"

Two days later the President of the Parole Board informed Jessie that his request for parole had once again been denied. The warden of the prison dismissed Mary Sue Lewis. When asked why she was being let go, she was escorted into the warden's private office and told why, and a strong suggestion was made that she should drop any further enquiries and move on with her life, somewhere other than anyplace in Vermont.

Side Note: I guess I have one of those faces that make people want to tell me things just so they can get things off their chest. Or maybe it is because I have a trusting face and they believe me when I say I will not tell anyone. All that is probably true, except I cannot keep a secret. I have to tell my best friend whatever I have heard in confidence. Trouble is my best friend keeps changing. All that is not important in regards to what follows because Mary Sue just sort of blurted everything out and not once did she tell me not to repeat to anyone to what really happened. For propriety sake I have changed the names of those involved. I am sure the censors at the University Press would make me do so anyway – end of side note.

Jessie was a pretty good art forger, but he never was able to paint pictures of faces from memory very well. When the picture was shipped to Oak

Dale the photographs he took, so he could replicate
the painting, did not come out very well, especially
the faces of Mary and one of the shepherds in the
background. He decided that since the archives
were hardly ever visited and seldom were the
pictures seen it would not be noticed that he used
Mary Sue's face as the model for Mary and the
president of the parole board for the shepherd.

Because Tim had been interviewing both
Mary Sue and the board president extensively
he saw the likeness on Steven's archive pictures
taken during the audit. He just put two and two
together. The two Irishmen were somewhat savvy
politically and realized that a scandal might occur if
all were known. They both went to see their cousin
the governor who was in the middle of his own
problems like most Vermont governors had been of
late, and he just told them to "fix it."

The brothers informed the parole board
president that it would not look good for his name
to be tied to such an embarrassing situation and the
church in Oak Dale didn't need the notoriety either.

They next went to see the warden and
suggested that they knew deep in their hearts, and
so did the governor who appointed him to that
position, the prison was in good hands and that the
warden would never have been so lax as to allow
such fraternization to take place, let alone escalate

to what might as well have been a prison break. The warden saw their logic and veiled threat. He then called Mary Sue to his office.

"So what are you going to do now?" I asked Mary Sue.

"I heard they have an opening for a correctional officer in a youth boot camp in Oklahoma. I am going to try my luck there. I did manage to wrangle a letter of recommendation from the warden. I sure will miss Jessie, however."

I was sure she would.

4

The Greatest Little Show on Earth

It was a circuitous route, given the fact that our final destination was to be almost due west of where we started, but after we left Bing Bang we headed south to Mo Mo, Pennsylvania. We stopped only long enough to pick up a small group both in quantity and dimension. It did not take me very long to decide who would be my next interviewees – midgets, dwarfs, or should I say little people, have always impressed me.

Many people get dwarfs and midgets mixed up. Midgets are just small people whose dimensions are proportional, while dwarfs are small people with some body parts out of proportion. I have the highest respect for them as groups. I have known a few that have been obnoxious and just plain mean, but they have been a minority of a small minority. For the most part little people are courageous and strong willed. They have great sagacity and are usually highly intelligent. I am pretty sure how I would face life if a chair hit my midsection or I had to buy my clothes off the children's rack, and it would not be with- out a lot of self pity on my part. So exploring why a group of little people would be boarding a train certainly would add some flavor to my venture.

At the same time I saw the wee folks get on the train, it dawned on my that Donnie had once again left the train for just a few minutes and then scampered back on just as we were pulling out of Mo Mo station. It had to have something to do with that lady friend of his, I surmised.

I hurried to where I thought the little peoples' car would be, thinking it would probably be the caboose since it was the smallest in area on the train, but as it turned out I was wrong and what further turned out being wrong was that I needn't have hurried.

While in Mo Mo, an additional customized observation car had been attached to our west bound locomotive. It was modified into sleeping quarters with a small dining room. One of the wee folks must be very well off.

I was unable to enter the added observation platform because a security guard whose name tag identified him as Ronald blocked the way. He wasn't very small in fact he was more closely related to that giant fellow in the Harry Potter books. I explained to the not- so-jolly giant who I was, but he did not answer so I figured what I said must have fallen on deaf ears. I was about to escalate my pitch when he told me to write my name down and what I wanted and that perhaps Mr. Smally would contact me in the morning. To my credit and physical well-being I managed to stifle a laugh when I heard the name of what must have been the head little guy. I wrote down who I was, what I wanted, what I wanted it for, and handed it over to an extended, enormous black hand.

It was a short ride to our next stop, Alacart, Pennsylvania. There we made a scheduled sidetrack lay-over, one that would last until the next afternoon. Ascertaining that the leader of the band of little people would not honor me with his presence until the morrow, I decided to explore the town of Alacart.

After bumping into one of my cabin mates several times, I forget which one, I managed to change into some comfortable walking shoes and slacks and headed out to see if I could find Donnie to accompany me, but Donnie was nowhere to be found.

Alacart was the boyhood home of Malcolm Delaney. Delaney was the first artist to cast bronze

statues of Spanish War Veterans. He was also
the sculptor who did the great statue of Teddy
Roosevelt and his Rough Riders charging up
San Juan Hill that adorned the front yard of the
White House while Teddy was President. It was
removed by President Wilson as being an eyesore
and relocated back in Alacart. It became the town's
main tourist attraction. Not too many people knew
about Delaney or his work, especially the large San
Juan Hill piece, but the people of Alacart were glad
to have it.

The train station was close to the heart of the
city, and like most tourist towns there were plenty
of souvenir shops and small eating establishments
surrounding the square and along Main Street.

It was my great fortune to be there during the
San Juan Hill Day parade. The Delaney-Roosevelt
High School band led the procession, followed
by the grand marshal, who claimed to have been
a rough rider, or so the side of his wagon stated.
Next came the local United States Army Reserve
Postal Unit that did their weekend drills in a small
armory just at the edge of town once a month.
Then came the combined VFW and American
Legion contingent followed by the reserve auxiliary
ambulance corps. I thought that was considerate.
There was a series of church floats; I thought the
Methodists had the most inspiring. The five piece
tambourine and bugle group from the Salvation

Army was very impressive, as was the newly acquired army surplus fire engine of the volunteer fire department whose siren worked very well and was demonstrated with enthusiasm. There must have been twenty horses ridden by men and women all dressed up to look like Teddy Roosevelt. They brought up the rear.

After the parade I slipped into a small diner and ordered some pickle bread that resembled a pizza. It was not bad at all, rather tasty I thought. I flushed it all down with several bottles of the local microbrew IPA. I managed to find my train and little sleeping compartment and did not awake until I felt the train moving again.

As I was breakfasting in the dining car nursing a minor hangover, Mr. Julian came up to me and asked if a Mr. Archibald Smally could join me. As I nodded a slow and curious consent, Mr. Julian stepped aside and a little person dressed in a three piece suit appeared. Rather dapper was he. Although his physicality was small, he exuded power and the nonchalance of wealth. I immediately stood and shook his hand as he sat himself opposite me.

Before I could figure out a way to begin my interview, Mr. Smally said, "Let me help you, son. The people accompanying me are family members or what is left of them. They are mostly nieces and

nephews along with a couple of second cousins. I
never married. I am taking them all to Los Angeles
for a reunion, a family reunion of sorts. And yes, I
designed the car myself, and yes, I am rich, and yes,
at one time I was famous. You are not old enough
to have ever heard of me and neither are most of the
members of what is left of my family. I organized
the reunion so my family could meet several of my
own little bands of brothers from bygone years. I
want to pass on the family heritage and have them
listen to the stories about what it was like to be a
small person in the old days from someone other
than myself. I have always thought that you are
today because of who was who and what one's
own whos did in the past. You see I was one of the
original munchkins in the Wizard of Oz. If you
look real close you can read my name in the credits
at the end of the movie. There are only a few of us
left, and I happen to be the oldest one of the bunch.
Before that I had a very successful career only
related a wee bit to theatrics."

I was stunned. I was sitting across from history,
my own history at that. One of my first childhood
memories was looking forward each spring for the
Wizard of Oz to come on television. I cared less
what he might have done prior to being around the
great Oz or what he did afterwards. I really did not
know what to say, so I did what I usually do when I
find myself in such mentally awkward situations and
said something asinine. "I bet you have received a

lot of royalties from as many times as that movie has been played and that is how you got rich."

"No, young man, I have never received one dime after the movie was shot. The producers took care of that."

"Well I'll be! That would not have happened today, I bet," said I, still not knowing exactly what do say next. I guess I was a little starstruck.

"No it would not," came a rapid reply.

"Did you stay in the theatrical world? I mean, did you ever act in another movie or something like that," I queried.

"No. I took the money they paid me and bought a ranch in upstate New York and raised horses. I was too old to return to my previous occupation. I was very successful in my new one. Although we never finished higher than fourth when we entered the Kentucky Derby, my stable's reputation was good enough to charge a lot for stud fees. I also developed a state of the art method of artificial insemination using my own patented equine sperm catcher."

I had never heard of an equine sperm catcher before, so he went on to explain, "When you want to draw semen from a horse you make it think it is about to mount a mare. Then you quickly place the sperm catcher in such a position to catch the fluid that spews out. My device was revolutionary because as soon as the horse's juice shot into the container, the semen was pumped through tubes that had been previously attached into a portable device that immediately froze the liquid in place, thus making it immediately ready for transport.

"It was very close work and required agility, so I always hired little people to do the work under the horse; most were one time acrobats from traveling circuses or retired pro wrestlers. I eventually got family members involved, and the rest is history. I invested my money wisely as did most of my employees, and, well, let's just say I am pretty comfortable now and so are my former workers and family members."

Naturally, raising horses that ran in the Kentucky Derby was interesting, let alone a horse sperm contraption manipulated by agile little people; but the whole concept was just a little too much for me to wrap my head around. I was much more interested in asking about the making of the Wizard of Oz. .

Me: What was Judy Garland like?

Mr. Smally: Distant but nice enough. Never smiled much.

Me: The Tin Man?

Mr. Smally: A very nice guy, as were Ray Bolger and the Cowardly Lion. They even taught me a dance step now and then.

He went on to tell the story about how all the munchkins protested what they were being paid and made the studio heads re-shoot the scene where every one was singing about the witch being dead. You can easily recall some of the lyrics "ding, dong the witch is dead, etc." Mr. Smally claimed that he and a few others encouraged the group to replace the word 'Witch' with the word 'Bitch' which was not noticed until after the scene was shot. The producers and directors hustled around and reassembled the group for another take which cost them more, especially in labor because they, the munchkins, were in a pretty good bargaining position.

Oddly enough, Mr. Smally said that the good witch was a real bitch and the wicked witch was the nicest one on the whole crew. "I didn't like Toto at all. He pissed on my leg once when I had to dress up like a flying monkey."

Since Mr. Smally and his family were going to be on the train till the end of the line, we were sure we would meet again and "next time young fellow

I want to hear more about this village archeology discipline. Sounds interesting. Like to read the last three books the university printed on the subject. I might be able to add a footnote that you would find interesting."

5

Homecoming and Going

Our next overnight stop was to be Rainsville, Ohio, Mr. Julian's childhood home.   The one thing I had found out so far about the Portland Express was that they were not in a real hurry to get anywhere.

Mr. Julian invited me to have dinner at the family compound just a little ways out of town. It was a refurbished antebellum mansion, and the food prepared by the family chef, he assured me, would be unparalleled. I was sure he was looking for some free publicity about the orchard operation just in case I decided to put any information about the place in my narrations. As you can tell, he did and I have.   .

Mr. Julian's younger brothers, twins Thomas and Jefferson, had acted as co-family patriarchs since their father died several years ago and together they took me on a tour of what now had grown to be apple, peach, and cherry orchards and an experimental vineyard. Mr. Julian stayed behind to visit with his wife at his house on the estate. I was dutifully impressed by the tour.

We ate lunch in the main dining room decorated in colonial style to accent the antebellum outside. The tavern attached to the dining room led to where apple cider and condiments were prepared and where, hopefully, future wine would be made. Next to that was a smokehouse, and better smoked meats and barbeque I had never tasted and have not tasted since. As far as dessert went, the peach cobbler was excellent, the cherry pie was sweet with just the right touch of sour, and the apple pie was strewn with a type of cinnamon that I had never encountered. I usually never eat three desserts, but Thomas and Jefferson insisted, and I was glad they did.

The twins suggested we retreat to Abe's, as they called Mr. Julian, for some illegally obtained Cuban cigars and strong Colombian coffee laced with Brandy and Benedictine. How could I refuse?

There I met Mrs. Julian, whose name was Mary Todd, and their twin nieces, Dolly and Madison, both of whom were over six-feet tall. I ignored the trend I noticed in naming family members and only wondered what the rest of the clan names were, but not to be impolite I never asked. It was a delightful evening and ended way too soon. Thomas and

Jefferson arranged for a car to take Mr. Julian and me back to the train. I was pleasantly surprised when Dolly and Madison rode with us. I was even more pleased to learn they would both be riding to the end of the line. "It is a graduation gift from Uncle Abe," they said.

The girls had graduated from high school the preceding spring and both had received academic scholarships tied into an athletic scholarship in Volleyball for Dolly and Softball for Madison at the University of Oregon. Both planned on studying horticulture with designs on returning home and working in the family business. I wondered if they were to have the same kind of accommodations I had in my three-person room built for one and a half. I doubted it and was sure they would not have to sleep in shifts.

6

Play Ball

We stopped many times between Rainsville and our next prolonged layover in Milton, Illinois. Somewhere along the line we picked up this older looking gentleman. He was sitting on the observation deck across from me, and he looked like he had a story or two by the lines imbedded deep in his face.

His name was Chester Eddy. His face and body seemed old but his voice had a deep baritone quality like he had been a radio announcer at one time. Which, in fact, he had I soon learned. I told him what I was doing on the train and asked him if we could talk a little. He was more than happy to oblige. He said he had been the play-by-play announcer for the Chicago Cubs, St. Louis Browns, and the Milton Mad Dogs. I confessed I had never heard of the Milton Mad Dogs, and he just laughed and said most people hadn't either. "They were a

short-lived farm team for the Brooklyn Dodgers.
Where they played is much more famous than they
were, at least locally. In fact, that is where I am
headed now, to the dedication of the field where
my announcing career began. Why don't you
come along with me? You might find something
interesting to put in that book your professor
wants."

About then Donnie came by. I really didn't
have anything to say to the poor sap, but he looked
sort of forlorn so I asked him to join Mr. Eddy and
me. He declined and said he had to wire his girl
some more money but said he would be up for
dinner that evening. He then scurried towards the
telegraph office.

As we walked out of the Milton train station we
were met by a television reporter and cameraman.
The interview was short and brief and to me seemed
cryptic, or at least I could not quite understand
what exactly was being said. I stood out of camera
shot far enough that I heard only bits and pieces of
the interview.

We were shown to a limousine and driven to
the side of a hill about three miles away. There
the mayor of Milton posed with Mr. Eddy in front
of a large curtain and presented him with a large
decorative key. Then, with overgrown scissors,
they both cut a rope that was holding up a curtain

blocking our view up the hill. As it dropped down, there was a table, microphone, and a large switch box. The small crowd that had assembled started counting down from 10 and when they reached 1, Mr. Eddy flipped a switch and light bulbs lit up across the hill. I was sort of puzzled at what first looked like random lights lit up on the side of a grassy hill but then I started noticing a pattern to the lights and things fell into place.

Punch and cookies were served, and hands were shaken. The limousine drove us back to the train station where we just barely made our connection. It was about dinner time, so I asked Mr. Eddy to join Donnie and me, but I wasn't sure the kid would be there. To my surprise he was already in the dining car waiting.

"You should have gone with us, Donnie, it was very interesting. I bet you have never heard about such a thing," I said.

"Well, you are probably right. Why don't you tell me about it now; then I will tell you the good news."

"You know, I think I will let Mr. Eddy tell you. You know, sort of like an original source since he was there and all, and it is more or less about him anyway. That alright with you, Mr. Eddy?"

"Sounds good to me. You know much about baseball, kid?" he asked Donnie.

"No, I played it a little at school but Montana wasn't really into baseball. Now and then one of my cousins would pick up a game over the radio when we would have a sleepover."

"Well then, you have an inkling and can picture what I am about to tell you easier than most. The city of Milton never had a real baseball team. A couple of the factories had some boys who played each other, and even the police department fielded a team now and then, depending on who was locked up on any given game day, and they could get a writ from the judge to let a particularly good player out for a while.

"One day the hardware store manager realized he had an excess of light bulbs. Also, because of an ordering mishap, some were even a different color from white. The owner's brother-in-law said he had heard about a lighted baseball field in Kansas City. The owner of the hardware store said that was nice but they didn't need to light up a baseball field because they had no baseball team in town, at least not one that people would pay to watch. "You ain't got my drift," the brother-in-law said and he proceeded to explain his statement.

"The two men approached the power and

light company and explained their plan and asked if the P&L would run a power cable to the base of Sagmore Hill just outside of town. The power and light manager said yes.

"They next went to the radio station, explained their plan and asked if they, WACK, would donate the necessary loud speakers and provide a feeder line to the announcer's booth.

"WACK thought it was such a great idea they said they would even provide the announcer."

Mr. Eddy seemed to be growing weary of doing all the talking so I took over.

"To make this story a little shorter, the brother-in-law and store owner put light fixtures on the side of Sagmore Hill roughly resembling a ball diamond. Each light represented a base, ball, or player. The offensive players were in yellow, bases were white, the ball was lit in red, and the defensive players were in royal blue.

"The radio station would pipe a game being broadcast over the wire to the announcer sitting behind a switch box at the base of Sagmore Hill. When a play was described on the radio that only the announcer could hear, he would flick a switch and the play would be replicated on the hill via lights to the thrill and enjoyment of the crowd. The announcer had to be quick of finger and tongue. Like if there was a man on base, there would be three lights lit and shown to the crowd – yellow, white, and blue – along with the red ball in the hands of the white pitcher, and he had to describe all of this while flicking switches in a timely manner. Just imagine what it would be like if the bases were loaded and a yellow batter hit a red ball to a blue player who threw to a white base and blue player. Well, you can get the gist.

"That is where Mr. Eddy came into the picture. The station owner selected Mr. Eddy, here, for the job. Mainly because none of the older guys around the station wanted the position. They thought the job was all hogwash and a real career killer.

"Mr. Eddy had a great radio voice and the quickest fingers anyone had ever seen. Milton town folks attended every game broadcast and were mesmerized by the dexterity manifested against the side of a sea green field.

The radio station sold more ads, the hardware store depleted their over supply of light bulbs and ordered more, and the kilowatts sold by the Power and Light Company increased dramatically. Everyone was happy.

"A scout for the New York Yankees was stranded in Milton one evening because of track repairs. There was a game being broadcast that night, so out of boredom he decided to attend. He had seen such a baseball display before but he had never seen or heard the likes of Mr. Eddy.

"One year later, the Yankees sent a farm team to Milton and hired Chester Eddy to do the play by play over live radio. They were called Milton Mudflaps. The Mudflaps were sold to the Yankees' cross town rival, the Dodgers, who eventually changed the Milton team to the Mad Dogs. They, in turn, were sold to another franchisee and then to another until the entire team was disbanded. Mr. Eddy stayed with the Yankees for awhile but then went on to the Browns, Cubs, and a short stint with the Dodgers.

"Mr. Eddy become very well known to industry insiders and went on to become one of the premier sports announcers of his day. And it all started right here in Milton. Ain't that right, Mr. Eddy?"

"Yessir, you got it about right. Now if you two gentlemen would excuse me, I think I need to take a nap."

As Mr. Eddy shuffled his way to the sleeping car Donnie and I ordered dinner. We sat there in silence for awhile then he said that he was ready to share some good news.

"Well, it is good news, but it sits upon some bad. My gal's mother was taken to the hospital for an emergency gallbladder removal. She did not have any money so my sweetie had to give her the money I gave her for the ticket to Portland. The good part of it is that she said that there was a sale on bus fares starting tomorrow that went right through Ulysses and that she could meet me there and meet my parents also. It just so happens my navy pay will be deposited in my regular checking account tomorrow when the tickets go on sale. I sent her my debit card number and password so she could take advantage of the sale. Isn't that just a great coincidence? Doesn't the Lord work in mysterious ways?"

I excused myself with the best smile I could muster and told him that was wonderful and headed to the club car thinking I wasn't so sure it was the Lord working in mysterious ways in this particular occasion.

7

Jesse James Slept Here

We rumbled west across the Mississippi River
and into a sea of corn most people called Iowa. We
pulled in to the Fort Sanctuary, Iowa, train station
early the morning after my conversation with
Donnie. The Portland Express would have at least
a three- hour layover, so I stepped out front of the
train station to see what the town looked like.

Fort Sanctuary was a normal looking
Midwestern town with one long main street with
shops and restaurants on each side. There was one
stop light that kept the north/south traffic from
bumping into those taking passage on the east/west
road.

As I was surveying the village township, a
double deck bus pulled up in front of the station.
On the side of the bus was a placard advertising
a village tour. As I was reading the sign it was
announced over the bus PA system that the cost of

the tour would only be three dollars and last one
hour at most. I got on board with several others
who needed to kill a little time. This was fine with
me because I would be able to scrutinize my fellow
sightseeing passengers and ascertain who I would
like to interview next. It did not take me long to
make my selection.

I took a seat on the top deck next to an older
gentleman who looked familiar. It took me a
minute to realize I had seen him plenty of times in
the dining car. He was a nondescript looking fellow
always in casual dress – but not now. Now he was
decked out in cowboy regalia, complete with a
ten gallon hat, chaps, vest, boots and a six shooter
hanging from his waist. We sat there in silence with
only a head nod of greeting and recognition while
the tour guide started her banter.

I was the one who broke the silence. My wild-
west looking bus companion, as I learned, was
Ralph Whatley, Ph.D. He told me he liked to dress
in the period of the place he was doing research
about and he was almost ready to finish a book
concerning Fort Sanctuary but needed one more
visit to put together some loose ends.

I had always thought that next to archeologist
and sociologist, Ph.D. history professors came a
close third on the scale of quirkiness. Dr. Whatley
was an interesting guy, regardless. I asked why Fort

Sanctuary was of such interest to him. So he told me as I am telling you now.

Fort Sanctuary was the earliest and furthest Catholic western trading post north of what is now the Minnesota/Iowa border. It got its name because the Jesuits who built a mission there offered forgiveness of sins once confessed. "Go and sin no more" was the last thing many a mountain man heard a white man say and soon forgot.

As the years went by and some sort of order settled on the northern plains, there were still a lot of adventurers needing forgiveness for acts that were deemed unacceptable in polite society. The Jesuits would grant pardons for sins, but the local authorities would not, that is, until two like-minded men from different backgrounds became elevated to positions of authority.

The army built a fort next to the mission and trading post. The name 'sanctuary' was tacked on to the end of fort and eventually everyone started calling the little community Fort Sanctuary.

The first commanding officer at Fort Sanctuary arrested anyone who even looked like they might be trouble and kept a close eye out on the wanted posters that made their way through town. Forgiveness of sins he did not care about, and sanctuary was out of the question.

The Jesuits went to hiding the bad guys after confession until they could sneak them out of town. The Abbot noticed that while the so called bad guys were in the mission they behaved like real law abiding citizens. They all helped with the chores needed to run the mission and attended mass daily. It was when they left the confines of the mission walls did they revert back to skullduggery.

Major Nelson was sent to replace the first commander, and being a devout Catholic he understood the rite of confession. But he was also a practical man. Laws had to be obeyed, and those who broke the law had to pay for their crime. It was his job to enforce the law within his jurisdictional area of responsibility.

The Major and Abbot became friends over cognac, cigars, and chess. They enjoyed each other's banter and respected the view of the other. They were both impressed by the other's ability to change his mind on a certain position if the other could make a sound argument for doing so. That is the backdrop of how Fort Sanctuary became a real sanctuary during the tenure of Major Nelson and Abbot Mosier.

Both men agreed that Jesus wanted sins to be forgiven. How many times do you forgive a sinner the Major enquired? Seventy times seventy was always the answer from the Abbot. Can you arrest a bank robber who robbed a bank in Chicago, the Abbot wanted to know. "No, that is a state crime, I represent the federal government" the Major would answer. "I could detain him, I guess, or put him on a train back to Illinois."

"What if he was truly sorry and said he wanted to start a new life?"

"How would I know he would keep his promise and was sincere?"

"What if you could keep track of him on a daily basis?"

An agreement was struck. The Major told the Abbot that he would look the other way if a man, or woman, made a confession and decided to make their home in Fort Sanctuary. No matter what written warrant or wanted poster was out there somewhere, the confessor would truly indeed be granted sanctuary within the confines of the city limits. However, if any of the repentant folks did anything to break the law while an official resident of Fort Sanctuary, the Major would arrest the villain at the first opportunity and show no mercy.

After the agreement, word soon spread throughout the outlaw community. If you were tired of being a criminal and tired of running from

the law and didn't want to go to jail, Fort Sanctuary
might just be the place for you. Some of the older
outlaws looked upon the situation as a Godsend,
which in fact it was. However, more bad guys
started showing up than was anticipated. Like
everyone else who works hard at their job, they too
needed some rest and relaxation. At Fort Sanctuary
they knew they could go to sleep at night without
fear of being arrested in the morning just for the
price of an "I'm sorry" in a booth in the corner of
the mission. If they changed their mind later and
left town and continued their hedonistic ways, well,
a smart man can always change his mind. Besides,
forgiveness is seventy fold, they could always come
back again and say they were sorry for what they
had been doing and for leaving last time, or at least
so they reasoned.

Word of Fort Sanctuary spread through the
lawman community also. Some decided it wasn't
a bad idea to hang around the outskirts of town
waiting for the bad guys to enter or leave. It got to
be a real contest of who could outwit or outfox the
other, with the bad guys usually getting the upper
hand.

One frustrated sheriff suggested a posse should
be formed and then sweep into town and arrest
the villains anyway, regardless of the Abbot and
Major. Others thought that was not a real good idea
because as one marshal said, "the army got more

guns than we do." Others thought that the Abbot might excommunicate them if they were part and party to such behavior. Most were not Catholic, but they were practical men and did not want to take the chance of never seeing heaven.

As the debate between the lawmen raged, word somehow leaked back to the mission and fort. The Abbot and Major rode out to where the lawmen camped and had a sit down. They explained the situation pleasantly enough but did remind the good guys very subtly that, yes, the army had a lot of guns and that God would not be pleased with anyone violating a religious proclamation.

The Abbot and Major did extend an olive branch. They said they had assurances from the titular head of the bad guys that if the good guys wanted to come into town for their own little vacation, peace would prevail. "Look at it as an intelligence operation," argued the Major. "You hang around town and try to pick up information as to who is coming and going and when and what route is to be used. Our edict and proclamation is only good in Fort Sanctuary. We don't want bad guys running around the countryside. Our theory is as long as they are here in Fort Sanctuary living under the rules we have established they are not a threat to anyone. But we are not naive enough to think after they leave here they will not fall into their old habits." The lawmen agreed.

Within few days it was not uncommon for
Pete "the Pistol" Swagger to play cards with Federal
Marshall McMillan at a saloon owned by the
notorious Al "the Vet" Andrews. Jesse James was
often seen playing pool with Bat Masterson, and
Cole Younger liked to toss darts with Sheriff Sam
McGreevy. Bloody Bill Anderson and William
Bonnie often threw horseshoes behind the saloon
owned by Wild Bill Hickok. Even the Abbot let
John Brown give a sermon at the mission once. It
was a diverse town and considered one of the safest
towns in the territory.

A few hundred miles to the east, Sister Mary
Alice heard God talking to her one evening after
prayers. He told her to form a sisterhood to assist
the Jesuits in bringing healing and spiritual guidance
to the western territory. Father McGee was so
delighted with the Sister's enlightenment that he
helped recruit other neophytes to the Western
Order, as it was to be called. There was no age limit
for joining the WO, so many a spinster and some
widows joined up immediately. Father McGee
knew who the most likely in his parish were to wed
so he actively recruited the others. An outsider
might have thought that Father McGee heard the
calling also, but he was more concerned with getting
rid of Sister Mary Alice. She had become a real
thorn in his side. The sooner she left the church
for points west, the happier he would be, and still

happier if she took as many of her like-tempered followers as would fit on a wagon.

Three official nuns and ten volunteers hopped in a wagon and followed the North Star. After a few weeks of traveling, the group took a leap of faith and for no reason turned left at a fork in the road and took one of the trails for no other reason than it looked less traveled than the other.

A few days later as the group was coming over a rise they noticed a village below at the base of the slope. They thought that would be a good place to spend the night, perhaps even get a bed and bath. At that same moment, a thunderstorm swooped down from the north and caused the women to huddle under the tarp covering the top of the wagon. They were watching the windblown rain slide sideways across the grass and then the clouds parted and the sun shone, casting a golden yellow brilliance over the village.

The rain stopped. Sister Mary Alice told her group that the hamlet below would be their home to do His work. She led her band of sisters into town.

The Jesuit Abbot was a smart man, a very smart man as were and are all Jesuits. However, being smart and being able to stand up to a woman with a mission who got her guidance straight from God is more than most men can handle. Even Major

Nelson found it hard to deal with Sister Mary Alice.

Sister Mary Alice was a domineering strong lady, and being the right hand of God just underscored her ability to be right and have no doubts about it. She was just as smart as any Jesuit and mentally alert and morally straight as any soldier. She was also dogged when she put her mind to something – she was no wimp. Her followers liked to recount an incident with a church elder at a parish picnic. The elder told everyone at the parish picnic that all nuns shaved their heads. He said he knew that for a fact. Many people had suspicions the elder's statement was accurate but none ever dared asked if it were true or not. When Sister Mary Alice got wind of what Elder Even was spreading around she confronted him and told him to take back what he said. He made the mistake of saying he would not take anything back and reached for her headpiece to prove to everyone he was correct. Before anyone knew what was going on, including the elder, he was lying flat on the ground with Sister Mary Alice straddling him with her knees on his shoulders thumping him on his chest with her right knuckle middle finger. She did this until he yelled out for all to hear that he had made it up about nuns shaving their heads. During the fracas, Sister's headgear stayed intact so the real question of baldness was not really answered for the skeptics. No one pointed that out, however.

Sister Mary Alice and her WO followers were successful in recruiting funds and labor in building their quarters. Outlaws and some lawmen may be scoundrels, but they all had mothers and sisters and so the Sisters, as they became known – albeit only three actually were - asked for assistance; it was immediately provided. The WO headquarters was completed in no time at all. The lawmen seemed to be someplace else whenever the bad guys would leave town and come back if it had been put through the intelligence cycle that the coming and going was for the completion of the structure. The soldiers, good guys, bad guys, and band of sisters worked side by side for the common good. Even some of the saloon girls asked to join the order, which delighted Sister Mary Alice, albeit depressed some of the men. However, when a bunch of men and women work together for an extended period of time, a dalliance or two takes place. Sometimes more than one or two, if the circumstances are right.

Well, the long and short of it is that given the fact that most of the soldiers who were stationed at Fort Sanctuary were misfits and not on anyone's list of most desirable, they were not choosy men. The members of the Western Order were frustrated spinsters who had never and wanted to, widows who had and still wanted to, and young unattractive girls who had not and thought they might. Ugly men and horny women make for a combustible combination.

One after another of the band of sisters would leave the order and marry a trooper or one of the truly repentant bad guys. With that came children and those who were becoming pillars of the community thought that the bad guy/good guy thing had gone on long enough and thus campaigned for its extinction. Such a place is no place to raise a family was the unofficial mantra.

Sister Mary Alice and her Western Order campaigned to rid the village of the undesirables unless they were truly repentant and had made a healthy contribution to the betterment of the village. Major Nelson received a new appointment and a promotion and moved further west. Abbot Mosier sequestered himself in the monastery and became a true monk not of this world. The mission was later taken over by the dioceses out of Minneapolis and a regular priest was sent to lead the flock. The new priest kept offering forgiveness but succumbed to the edicts of the new military governor of the area and did not offer sanctuary.

Fort Sanctuary became an average town with average people going about their average lives with an above average crime rate. It was not until a joint task force of Minnesota and Iowa historians started looking into old files saved from a fire at the old mission did the past – the experiment, if you so choose to call it – came to light. Dr. Whatley was saving the past from obscurity and extinction. It sounded a lot like he was practicing Village Archeology to me.   Professor Simpson thinks he invented the discipline. I can't wait to tell him about Dr. Whatley.

8

Peter Piper

Some think that Pickle Ball started in California like all fads and fantasies. Not so. Pickle Ball originated in Ireland. The Irish, in a particular area of Ireland – a small community called Devere, where Pickle Ball originated, happened to be shorter than the normal Irishmen. The people of Devere found it difficult to maneuver around a large tennis court. (Tennis had been introduced to Ireland from France by William the Green, the conqueror of most of Normandy. That is a little known bit of trivia that can come in handy at a parlor game.)

The size of a Pickle Ball court fits the anatomy of small people who are among some of its most ardent devotees. The court is about half the size of a tennis court, and small players can scurry around and get to the position they need to be without much trouble.

The English banned the game after conquering Ireland because it reminded them of the French game of tennis. Eventually, the game just sort of faded away, but not completely. There was always some fashion of the game brewing somewhere. It was brought over to the Americas and took the form of "wall ball", a game that the poor and underprivileged played against the backdrop of tenement housing.

It was not until a bunch of Irish railroad workers began reminiscing about the old country that several lads started piecing things together. One knew a little bit about some rules, another knew a little bit more, and several of the gandy-dancers came up with the size of the court.

Because of a breakdown in supply shipments, there was a week layover in the town of Green Vine, Nebraska, one summer. Instead of spending every waking hour in the local pub/saloon, which the townies expected of the Irish, the men decided to build a Pickle Ball Court.

The people of Green Vine watched in awe as the Irish sprang into action and constructed the court in less than a twelve-hour day. The lads starting playing and the people of Green Vine watched with interest. It wasn't long until one of the Irish invited a townie to play, then another and then another. The game became very popular with the town folk, so much so that when the supply problem was remedied and the crew packed to leave, a huge party was held, which happened to be on St. Patrick's sister's birthday, or so the Irish claimed.

Eventually, the rules were refined by the citizens of Green Vine while new courts were erected further down the line by railroad workers until they reached Portland. From there the game fanned out and started permeating the rest of the far west. Gradually, the game snaked its way back eastward but for many years did not take on the enthusiasm it had in Green Vine.

The whole game could have died out, but several things were happening in the American culture that saved the game from extinction. Golf was becoming more expensive, as were most leisure and not so leisure activities. People started retiring at an earlier age and wanted something to do other than crafts and cards. The Mayor of Green Vine, a transplanted marketing executive from Sacramento, started Dill Day to commemorate the start of the game. It was a huge success, and with the marketing connections of Mayor Gherkin, it received much notoriety. The resort areas picked up on the fad and paid attention when people making reservations would ask if they had Pickle Ball courts instead of shuffle board courts. It really started gaining popularity among the early retired – patricians and plebeians.

Mr. Oliver Basaltic was the one who educated me on the history of Pickle Ball. He was the first National Gold Medalist in the sport of Pickle Ball and helped to establish the Pickle Society, whose job it was to spread interest and develop pickle ball chapters throughout the United States. He claimed that they had chapters in every state in the Union, and Texas and California boasted more courts than any others.

Mr. Basaltic was asked to be the tournament's ceremonial host this year and the Grand Marshall at the annual Pickle Ball Day Parade. The annual date is always the first Saturday after the 17th day of March. According to tradition, that is the birthday celebration of St. Patrick's sister.

9

Lost and Found

When doing research that requires interviewing, I usually select someone who sticks out in a crowd. You know that type of person. The one you automatically pick out of a bunch of people for reasons that have not really been revealed though scientific research. Some call it charisma. My next interview, I decided, would be with the most nondescript person I could find on the train. I wanted to find the guy or gal who goes to a party and the next morning no one knows they were there, let alone remembers their name, if in fact it was ever known. He or she would be the same type who walked down the hall at work and eventually someone would want to know who the new person was only to find out that they had been working there for the last ten years.

There were plenty of people aboard the train who were not charismatic, but none so far that really fit what I was looking for. However I am dogged about such things and eventually, in the lounge car after sipping a Harvey Wallbanger, a little known but delicious and dangerous drink, I spotted my man sipping on what looked like a ginger ale.

After ensuring he was not waiting for anyone - you can always tell - I strolled over, fortified by Mr. Wallbanger, and introduced myself. (He was somewhat surprised because people like him rarely are approached by strangers on a train unless it is a Hitchcock film in black and white. Come to think of it, that didn't turn out so well did it? I digress, sorry. Must be the Harvey Wallbanger I just downed.) Surprised or not, he politely offered me a seat and even asked if he could buy me a drink. I declined because one HW is my limit except for that time at …, sorry there I go again. Anyway after introductions I told him I wished to interview him. I was flat out honest with him and said the Portland Rail Road Company was trying get a snapshot of their basic passenger list, etc., etc., etc., or yada, yada, yada. Take your pick. (Of course I did not tell him that I picked him because he was lacking in charisma and was nondescript. That would have required at least two more HWs.)

He did a short little chuckle and said, "I understand, young man, I retired from a marketing research public relations firm several years ago. I have analyzed a lot of the same type of data you are gathering."

I was somewhat surprised. His silent demeanor did not radiate that was the type of business he would be associated with. Before I could begin talking, about what I am not sure, he said, "I would love to see what data you have collected, but I know such things are confidential." However, confidentiality did not stop him from telling me about why he was where he was and what his mission was about.

His name was Arthur Smith. He was a widower with three grown children and six grandchildren – all of whom were moderately successful in their particular fields. His income was within such and such a range, he answered to Caucasian on census enquiries, and was in the upper of the age brackets listed on most forms. His favorite color was purple; he liked Johnny Carson and had a brother that was gay. "What else would you like to know?"

"Well, you sort of get my drift but what I really want to know is why you are on this particular train?"

With that question he became much more serious. "I am going to meet someone I have wanted to meet for a long time, and this train is the only public transportation that goes through Small Port, South Dakota, two stops up ahead if I read my timetable correctly. It ought to be interesting, considering the circumstances and the fact he does not know I am coming, or even that I exist."

I wanted to ask him more about his sojourn but before I could he told me the story. Everyone has a story but most never get to tell anyone because no one ever asks, especially if they are part of the nondescript.

When Mr. Smith was a young man in his middle twenties, he was partaking in the family deathwatch at a large regional hospital in the Midwest. He was closer to his grandfather than many grandkids, basically because Mr. Smith had lived with Gramps from the time he was four years old until he married twenty years later. He never mentioned why and I never asked why his mother and father were not part of the story.

Gramps was on his second stroke and things did not look good. The family, meaning, aunts and uncles and cousins, hung around the waiting room taking turns going in and visiting with Gramps. He never responded to any of the visitations, and the doctors said they didn't think he would be aware of any one's presence anyway but they were not really sure. So just in case Gramps was aware of what was going on outside his body, relatives took shifts and read to him eighteen hours a day. He was dearly loved by all in the family, so no one looked upon their attentiveness with resentment as some do-gooders end up doing when the goodness becomes a job and not a labor of love.

The family shared the waiting room with another family that was going through something very similar. There was a ten-year old boy who had been struck by an automobile and was hanging on to life by less than a thread but hanging on nonetheless, to the dismay of all the doctors. The small group would hold prayer vigils every hour, and their pastor would visit at least twice a day to pray and counsel the family.

While the little boy's group was solemn and prayerful, Gramps' group was somewhat more practical and thus less stressed. Gramps was old; he had led a hard but good life, and he had told all the family that he was ready to die whenever the good Lord thought it was time. One of Gramps' groups made a comment that went totally misinterpreted by a member of the young child's group. It was never really determined what was said by Gramps' group, but it was interpreted by the other group to mean that praying for God to save the little boy's life was a pretty dumb thing to do.

Arty, as they called Mr. Smith back then, was walking back to the waiting area from his turn reading to Gramps. The father of the boy approached Arty and said with tears in his eyes that he knew that God could take his son anytime He so chose, but he also knew that He could save his son if He so desired. "I trust in God and rely not on my own understanding," said the father.

Arty didn't know where his comment came from when he told the father in all sincerity, "Gramps is an old man, and he is ready to go. I don't know what you think was said, but believe me, no one in our family would make fun of anyone else's belief, especially in a situation like this. If it is any consolation, if God is keeping score or a tally sheet I hope he marks one up for the boy; Gramps is ready to go and we are ready to send him." The two men parted and never spoke again.

Gramps died later that night surrounded by friends and family. Gramps' group disbanded and reconvened once again at the funeral. No one mentioned the boy's group or what happened to the boy. As far as Arty knew no one even remembered the group they shared a waiting room with. Throughout his life Art, as he became known to his business associates, would wonder what had happened to the boy off and on throughout the years, but did no more than just that, wonder.

After Art retired he had a heart attack. Such events make one wonder a little more than normal. They wonder why they never did climb that mountain, took that extra day of vacation or spent more time playing baseball or dolls with their children. Sometimes they wonder if God saved a little boy because he heard Arty suggest that he should. He wondered if God thought it was a tradeoff, "you take Gramps and let the world have the boy."

Art had a full recovery from his heart attack. He engaged a private investigator to see if the boy of long ago had lived and if so where he was and what was he doing. Had the boy taken advantage of the trade that God had made, had the boy turned into a young man who did good things and did he live a good life by helping and loving others or…? But Art did not want to think about the "ors".

"So I guess you found the boy, or I guess he would be a man by now and living in Small Port," I said.

"You got that right son, and here is my stop."

"Good luck, Mr. Smith," I said and we shook hands. "God be with you."

"And with you," he replied.

As the train was pulling out of the station I saw Mr. Smith wave down a cab. I guess he knew where he was going because he had certainly known where he had been. Godspeed, Arthur Smith.

10

Donnie Update

As the train pulled out of Small Port and shot up towards Peculiar, South Dakota, I spied Donnie walking into the dining car. It had seemed like days since I had last seen him, but in reality it had only been a few hours. He strolled right up to my table where I was enjoying a delightful apple fritter that Mr. Julian's nieces had brought with them from the orchard. He asked if he could sit. Being the gracious person I am, I said yes and through a misdirection of sorts hid the last two fritters, lest he asked for one. I said I was of the gracious type, not that I could not be selfish when it came to apple fritters. So with a little sleight of hand learned from my days as a magician's assistant, they vanished. Come to find out there was no need for such trickery because Donnie was too distraught to notice. I braced myself for the next bit of penny opera.

"Sit, me fine lad, tell Uncle all about it." My cynicism went unnoticed.

"It is Lucy." Even though he had never mentioned his lady friend's name I knew exactly whom he meant. "Poor gal has such bad luck. She was about to give her two- weeks' notice at Butcher's when the star broke her leg falling from the pole. This left her boss in such a terrible predicament he begged Lucy to stay another two weeks. She felt so sorry for the guy and he had been so nice to her that she agreed. It really broke her heart having to miss out meeting my parents in Ulysses. She was going to surprise me. Problem is she had already given up her lease in her one room apartment and would have to sleep in the group dressing room at Butcher's. Butcher's is a twenty-four hour entertainment center and she would not be able to get much sleep. I didn't want her to do that, so I contacted my mom and dad and they are sending her some money to rent a motel room for the next two weeks. She doesn't even have an address so the money is going straight to Butcher's."

"I thought she had your bank account information." I said. "Why get your folks involved?"

"That is even more bizarre. She said the bank had made a mistake of some sort and my accounts, both checking and savings, show zero balances. I have to contact the Naval Finance Officer as soon as I get to Oregon. Poor, poor, Lucy. She was crying when she hung up the phone at our last stop. She was so upset."

I was becoming "so upset" also, but more around my stomach and wondering what I would do with the body if I ever made it back to Chicago.

11

A Peculiar Situation

I had never been in South Dakota and hope that I won't ever again. If you ever decide to go there, call me up and I will try to talk you out of it. No, I am just kidding. I heard something like that said about an auto instructional booklet once and have been waiting to work that into a narrative someplace and thought this would have been as good a place as any. I might be wrong, usually am, about such things, but anyway back to South Dakota.

South Dakota is a nice place and the people there are very pleasant as long as you don't take sides on a couple of issues. No, it is not the Bury My Heart at Wounded Knee kind of thing or if you support or don't support AIM or side with the BLM on most things. The couple of things that get you into trouble is where you fall on who ought to be the next face on Mount Rushmore and how did Peculiar, South Dakota, get its name. Or so the

lady mayor of Peculiar, South Dakota, Mayor Beth
Stinemeyer told me at my next interview.

The Mount Rushmore question, she admitted,
is just a matter of opinion with good arguments
as to who it should be. That will undoubtedly be
decided by a blue ribbon panel if in fact any other
head ever is planned to be carved there. "I, for one,
have no opinion on the matter," she confessed and
neither did I, having never seen the four already
there. I was more interested on the peculiar
Peculiar question.

According to the Lady Mayor, when the
railroad was picking refueling and overhaul stations
along the Portland to Portland route, it made sense
to erect the facility at a specific location due to the
logistics involved. Trouble was, there was no town
at that particular location and none for miles and
miles around. The engineers who did the planning
insisted that the spot they selected had to be at the
specific location they first suggested. They gave
good, sound reasons, so much so that the president
of the line, Samuel Hoginfessor, agreed and settled
the dispute by building a town with the assumption
that if "we build it they will come" and they did.

At first the town consisted of only railroad
employees but later it started attracting other sorts.
When President Hoginfessor was on an inspection
tour of his western facilities he naturally wanted

to see the town he had decided to build. He was embarrassed. That such a place was allowed to exist and was associated with his railroad mortified him. He knew that railroad builders could be crude, rude, and downright uncivilized, but when you threw in the types of men and women attracted to such places during the westward movement it made things more immoral than he had dreamed possible.

He instructed his underlings to clean the town up. "Do what you have to do to rid the evil around here and make this a place that one would be proud to have one's name associated with. I want this town to be an enclave of polite society, a beacon of western morality and cultural significance; do I make myself clear?"

It is said, but without proof positive verification, that the cleaning up of the town delayed the completion of the Portland to Portland by over a year, and many a recalcitrant went missing. During the cleanup period it was also rumored that Wild Bill Hickok and Calamity Jane helped rid the place of undesirables, along with some other hired people of the same ilk.

Finally the town was cleaned up and the railroad petitioned the state of South Dakota for incorporation, part of which was filing for United States Postal Status. To do so, the place had to be given a name other than the numbered engineer drawing that had thus far been its only designation.

The company thought that it would be best if the people who were working and living in the town and helped clean the place up be given the opportunity to make the selection as to the town's name. A committee was formed and eventually several names were selected as distinct possibilities.

Dakota City, West Junction, Silver, Platt, Port, along with the name of some civil war generals and Indian fighters and worthy presidents were some of the more reasonable names suggested. Of course there were always those who wanted something like Buffalo Gulch, Opossum Hole, Turtle Creek, etc. None had a majority, however.

The company decided it had to come up with a name, so some of the more career- minded executives decided it would be best to name the community after a president. All the execs agreed that a town called Hoginfessor sounded like a grand name.

A clerk at the Interior Department Land Use office thought the name Hoginfessor was sort of peculiar, and said so when he passed the request on to the Bureau of Duplicate Political Subdivision Names. The clerk there verified that no such city/ town by the name of Hoginfessor existed and the name in and of itself was not that peculiar. It was easy for him to so state because he was of the Pennsylvania Dutch tradition. Since there seemed to be a disagreement between agencies, the department responsible for interagency discrepancies was informed, but after careful analysis noted there was not really a problem and it was peculiar that such a problem was thought to exist. After an internal review the request was finally sent to the appropriate postal authority in charge of such things where it was authorized that the name Hoginfessor (even he thought the name was sort of peculiar) was to be used on all governmental documents and communications referencing that area from then on, regardless of its peculiar sounding name. He then informed the wire service to send a telegram informing the state officials as to what the name of the town was to be known as from here on out.

It was the telegram operator's first day on the job and he was eager to please so he immediately sent off the wire as fast as possible. He was not familiar with legalese nor with the slight speech impediment his immediate supervisor had.

The official notice sent to the community read in part: "THE NAME YOU SELECTED FOR YOUR COMMUNITY IS VERY UNIQUE STOP IT IS PECULIAR STOP."

Then without a pause the Lady Mayor said,

"Then of course there is the other side. Some think that the people who settled here were a bit odd from the get go, with all the railroad working types about and those who associated with them. Having such a less than desirable element, it seemed peculiar to those passing by that there were a lot of churches and opera houses about. It got to be commonplace when travelers would meet up after having visited here once and tell each other that it was certainly peculiar back there. The term peculiar caught on in the local vernacular and when something out of the ordinary occurred, people would say 'well that's peculiar for you.' The Daily Plains, a weekly newspaper in the territory, found out that the railroad was investing a lot of money in a new town in the area and was looking for a name. The headline on the edition of the paper writing about the situation read IT'S PECULIAR. One thing led to another and, well here you are and here I must get off."

As she was departing, I yelled after her, "Which story do you believe?" She yelled back over her shoulder, "Oh, I suspect there is a little truth in both. Ta, ta." A true politician through and through.

I sort of like the first story because much in history is determined by human folly, error, or design. That is what I like about Village Archeology. You never know if your conclusion is correct but no one can prove that it is not. Some things may not be true but if they aren't they sometimes should be. Society needs to leave things to the professionals like me to decide what should and should not be perceived as real or not. That's not peculiar is it?

12

Meat Loaf Madness

It has been said that the sandwich was invented by the Earl of Sandwich so he could eat and play poker at the same time. I am not sure about that. When contemplating such heavy subjects sometimes my mind wonders as to when the first that, or the first this was the first. Things just don't happen without there being a first. Take the deep underlying mystery of who invented the first meat loaf. The subject has thwarted historical scientific attempts to find the answer for years. Sometimes such discoveries are just right under our nose, so to speak, but go undetected.

If there was such a thing as a professional meat loaf taster like there is one for wine, then it would be me. So you can just imagine how elated I was when Mr. Julian asked me if I wanted to meet last year's winner of the Montana Meat Loaf Cook Off.

Simon, just Simon, as many consummate

professionals call themselves, (not that they call themselves Simon but they drop their first or last name for marketing purposes, I suppose) had just arrived on board. I knew nothing about the man, but if he won anything to do with meat loaf then he was the man I wanted to meet more than anyone else, at least at the present time.

Mr. Julian told me to come to the Chef's wagon around two in the afternoon. Simon was going to show the train cooks how to prepare what would become the Portland Express signature dish every time they crossed the border into Montana. It was the same recipe he had used to win last year's annual event. I was right on time.

Before Simon began his training session he had each person in the cook's car sign a nondisclosure document that swore us never to reveal in writing the ingredients and techniques used to prepare the dish outside of the confines of the Portland Express Company. "Academics are not exempt from such disclosure," he said, looking directly at me. I gave a slight nod of the head indicating I understood.

What I can tell you, however, is that the meat loaf lived up to its billing and was the best tasting meat loaf I ever had the pleasure of slipping between my two lips. The only disappointment was we were given only a sample, and the full portion would not be made available until we crossed back into

Montana from Idaho on our return trip. I decided that I wasn't going to fly home after all. The meat loaf had that much appeal.

The Montana contest was going to be held in Silver Bullet this year and Simon had been invited to be the "secret" judge. It was sort of an inside joke to all concerned. All the participants knew who the judge was to be but, for some reason lost to antiquity, the judge started wearing a mask. It was just traditional and like many traditions made no sense to anyone living but like most traditions no one seriously considered trying to change it either. The train had a four-hour layover which Mr. Julian insured me would allow plenty of time to attend the event.

Although Simon was a professional he traveled without any roadies. Mr. Julian had arranged for some of the night porters to help transport Simon's personal items but, wanting to ingratiate myself with the "Man", I volunteered to carry his valise. He seemed most appreciative.

As we were about to debark, Simon grabbed his left arm and fell to the floor. Having earned a red cross merit badge when I was a boy scout I recognized the heart attack immediately. So had one of the porters. Being swifter than I, he started performing CPR and gradually Simon started breathing normally, his color returned and he tried

to sit up. "I must continue; my public demands it."
Then he fainted.

Mr. Julian stepped in and took charge
and directed the porters to carry Simon to the
President's car and sent a conductor-in-training for
a doctor.

To this day I am not sure what came over me.
It must have been the long line of carnival folks I
had descended from and that one Victorian female
impersonator whose picture hung in my aunt's
house for years that made me do it. I instinctively
realized the show must go on. Simon and I were
about the same size so I donned the mask and
walked out of the train onto the platform, and
up the stairs to the stage where five meat loaves
awaited.

I was met with a thunderous ovation. How
grand, I thought to myself, it would be to have the
adulation of so many when having or done so little
in reality.

In front of each meat loaf was a man dressed in
a tuxedo. On his left forearm was draped a white
cloth napkin. Upon the napkin rested a fork held
in place by the tip of its prongs by the tuxedo-clad
man's right hand. It did not take me long to figure
out what to do.

After taking a bow and extending my arms to quiet the crowd, I approached meat loaf number one, took the fork and gently pierced the meat loaf to a bite size element and placed the morsel in my mouth. I looked towards the blue sky and squinted my eyes like I was deep in concentration. The crowd was silent. I then made a mark between one and ten on a note pad that had been placed next to each meat loaf entry. I immediately turned the paper over so no one could see what score was written down. I then proceeded to do the same thing at each meat loaf station.

As if I was trying to do a thorough analysis, I took the pads with the scores on them back to the dining car while the local band played a tune adapted for the occasion, titled 'Meat Me in St. Louis'.

As I entered the dining car I ripped off my mask and with sweat dripping from my brow, I saw Mr. Julian and Mr. Smalley and I asked in a horrified manner what I was supposed to do next. Surely the crowd would find out that the real Simon was in the hospital recovering, I hoped, from a heart attack.

Mr. Julian and Mr. Smalley were cool as cucumbers. One of them said, "That has all been taken care of," and the other said, "Simon was checked into the hospital under his real name and no one will ever find out."

"Won't he be upset that a pure amateur like myself made one of the more outstanding decisions that will forever be associated with his name?"

"I doubt that very much, young man," soothed Mr. Smalley. "Simon is a professional entertainer; anytime he can get any kind of credit he will grab it. Whether he did it or not is unimportant. The credit is what counts. Also he will never let it be known that he suffered some kind of coronary because then someone would draw a link between the consumption of meat loaf and his heart ailment."

"So, sir," Mr. Julian said, "go back on the stage make your selection and then faint. I have instructed the engineer to head out of town as soon as I give him the word. That young friend of yours, Donnie I believe his name is, will be the one who will carry you from the platform back onto train and yell just loud enough for the press to hear that you fell from exhaustion. Now move it, sonny boy."

I did what I was told and ran out on the stage with my mask replaced. I held up meat loaf number three indicating it took the day. I then collapsed into the waiting arms of Donnie, who carried me back into the dining car. As we made our escape from Silver Bullet I thought I heard a skeptical voice from the crowd saying, "Who was that masked man?"

13

Big Jake and Larry

We were coming up on Ulysses as I awoke. I was dreading this more than if I had to return to Silver Bullet on my way back to Portland east. (After my misadventure I had decided to fly.) Poor Donnie, I just knew his heart was going to be broken, that he was going to feel like a fool, become embarrassed when he finally figured things out and sink into a deep depression. Such things are not meant for our boys who wear the uniform. There should be a law against it. If I ever get elected president I am going to sign an executive order stipulating that it will "now and henceforth be unlawful to break the heart of a service person while he/she is on active duty." I am sure I would get the country's support.

I looked for Donnie everywhere up and down the train. He was nowhere to be found. I ran down Mr. Julian and enlisted his help. I was so frantic he first did not understand what I was talking about.

When it dawned on him why I was so hyper he said, "My friend, you need to take a breath, relax. There is nothing you can do; Donnie got off the train at our last stop. You slept through Ulysses.'

I breathed a sigh mixed with relief and resignation. I managed to do a silent Hail Mary and an Our Father. I then, like all good Catholics, ordered a Bloody Mary from the first passing steward.

As the train chugged along though a Montana mountain pass I noticed two hunter types sitting down across from me. "Son," said the larger of the two, "you look just like I reckoned I looked like once when I was confused and bewildered."

"Well, I don't know what you looked like then nor I now, but I am a little confused and bewildered; of course it could be my third Bloody Mary that moves my countenance around a bit."

"Come on, Jake," said the other man, "He don't seem the type. That conductor must have been wrong. I ran into this little guy in the observation car; let's go see him."

"No," Jake said sort of gruffly. "He works for the college and will write down stuff we tell him Ain't that right sonny?"

"Anything you say, old pal of mine." Haven't you noticed that alcohol makes a best friend or a worse enemy sometimes? You never know which way it will go when drinking with a stranger.

"Fine," said Jake, "Let us retire to the dining car, and we will tell you all about what we are planning to do. Perhaps you will be able to give us some legitimacy if we are published in a college journal or something akin."

After several cups of coffee and piece of apple pie from the Julian orchard, I was focusing much better. I explained to Jake and his big companion, named Larry, what the Portland Express Rail Road had hired the university to do. It took awhile for me to explain why something like archeology would be doing stuff other than digging in the dirt, but I eventually succeeded somewhat when Larry said, "It don't make no never mind. Go ahead, Jake."

Jake told me that he and Larry were the last two individuals to have seen Big Foot. I kept a stoic face and asked how did they know they were the last two to have done so. Jake produced a magazine. "We were interviewed in the Big Foot Weekly and it says that no other accounts have been forthcoming since our encounter four years ago." This notoriety, Jake said, made Larry and him want to track the legendary critter down and bring to the world proof positive that Big Foot existed.

Still managing my stoic expression I asked
in what I hoped was a serious sounding tone,
(remember I said these guys were real big) "Can
you describe the events leading up to the last time
you saw Big Foot?"

"We certainly can," and they did.

Jake and Larry had been hired by a lumbering
contractor to clear a trail back to a deserted lumber
camp in Idaho. Because there were Blue Nosed
Pickle Eaters nesting in some of the trees that might
have to be cut down and an almost extinct Horne
Rim Red Beetle, that produced hallucinogenic
dung and spent every other winter hibernating in
the bark of some green aspens, the EPA would only
allow the old camp to be reopened if no mechanical
equipment was used to blaze the trail from the
trail head to the camp. After the trail was opened,
inspected, and passed said inspection via EPA
guidelines, limited horse and wagon use would be
permitted to remove the lumber. It was a real labor-
intensive project, but the kind of pine they were
after was very expensive on the commercial market
and this was the first time EPA had allowed it to
be harvested, so there was some real money to be
made. (This was more than I wanted to know, but
I took notes to see if any of what was said could be
of use for background. Besides, I didn't think I had
won Larry over to my side. He kept looking at me

with an expression between disgust and irritation.
Remember I said he was a big man and I have
always felt like one should not make enemies with
big men, if one could help it.)

"Larry and I," continued Jake, "worked for
almost a month until we came within sight of the
camp. It happened to be on a Thursday before the
fourth of July on Sunday so we decided to take
a long weekend. We unloaded our road clearing
equipment from the horse drawn wagons and
readied a saddle horse and a pack mule for each
of us and headed towards civilization and a festive
holiday weekend.

"When we returned the following Monday, our
staging camp was a wreck. It looked like someone
had purposely destroyed our saws, chisels, and
axes, along with bits and bridle, and taken our
food supply that we had hung in trees to keep the
bears away. Larry and I were familiar with tracking
techniques and immediately started following a trail
left by the ones who had done the pillaging.

"Our path-finding took us straight into the
deserted camp and into what used to be the camp
bunkhouse. As we entered the bunkhouse we saw
three large hairy-looking creatures. The largest
of the three must have stood over seven feet and
looked even bigger when he expanded his chest and
gave out a roar that sent chills up my spine. The

next smaller creature did the same thing, but its scream was more chilling than the bigger one. As it made the frightened sound it slid the smallest creature to the rear.

"Taking a page from an old story an Eskimo once told me, I ripped off my shirt and told Larry to do the same and copy everything I did. We expanded our chests with as much air as we could, held out our arms to the side making a curling motion, opened our eyes wide, and slowly stepped backwards until we were out the door and out of sight of the beasts. We then turned around and ran as fast as we could back to our horses and rode like the wind to the Ranger's station several miles down the road."

"Well, that is a real interesting story but I hope you realize that to write anything down about your adventure that would be associated with the University I would need a little proof other than your word," I said, and then quickly added, "of course, I don't doubt you for a minute. (I did mention that they were big guys, didn't I?) I do have one question though, why did you take your shirts off?"

"That was to confuse Big Foot. You remember I said we made our eyes big also, well my old Eskimo friend told me that animals are not used to seeing other animals with more than two eyes. When we exposed our chests, Big Foot was confused because he thought our areolas were another set of eyes. That confused him long enough for us to make our escape."

"We understand about needing more proof than just what we said," chimed in silent Larry, "That is why we want you to come with us. You know, to add some viability and validity to our story. Even take a camera. I have no doubt we can find the family again."

The three of us discussed the matter and to my surprise both men seemed to understand my reasons for not going. There was the time factor involved, my train schedule, I didn't have the proper gear and clothes and all, etc. Of course the real reason was that I was afraid we might find Big Foot, and the three of us would be looked upon like everyone else who claimed to have found Big Foot, if we were able to escape being lunch. I think I sold the idea of not going when I gave Larry my University smart phone which operated via satellite. "When you do run across Big Foot and the family, take a picture of it, send to the phone number listed (It was Professor Simpson's) and then press the You Tube button. I am sure it will go viral and you both will be known world wide, just like Armstrong and Columbus."

Mr. Julian had the train stop near the base of

the mountain close to the logging trail they had
started to clear four years earlier. I watched as they
hiked towards fame up the side of the mountain that
would undoubtedly be named after one of them
someday. I knew they would find nothing. I realized
that their first encounter with Big Foot probably
came from being hallucinated accidentally by
sniffing beetle dung, but then no one would really
know for certain, would one? However there was
part of me that wanted to believe that they would
not only find Big Foot, but the log cabin Jimmy
Hoffa was staying in as the guest of D.B. Cooper,
who was writing an account of who really shot JFK
or maybe even JR with the help of space alien time
travelers.

14

Quatro

The train settled down to its click-a-tee-clack as we passed between Idaho and Washington. The train timetable I carried with me read that there would not be another stop, at least a scheduled stop, until we reached Portland. It was the longest part of the trip without interruption - no stopping, no sidetracking, no interruptions - that would prevent me from compiling my notes and maybe even allow me to start a first draft for Professor Simpson and the Portland Express marketing department.

To begin things properly, I ordered a double margarita with plenty of salt and ice, a basket of chips with salsa that could destroy the inside of an amateur's mouth, and cranked up my Joe Cocker CD. It was then that Mr. Julian and Mr. Smally ran down the hall followed by Ronald and braced me breathlessly.

Mr. Julian was dressed normally, but Mr. Smally was decked out in what can only be described as a "great white hunter" outfit complete with a brown pistol belt, tan shorts, knee socks and jungle boots, with a matching colored hat and silver handcuffs hanging from his belt. His bodyguard, Ronald, was dressed similarly but instead of the old time Jungle Jim hat, he wore a red fez. In one hand he held a leash attached to the neck of a bulldog - who resembled Mr. Smally - and in the other hand carried a long pole with a rope and a shotgun slung over his shoulder.

Mr. Julian immediately said, "Sir, there has been an escape from the Oregon State University Research Facility, and Mr. Smally has been asked to use his skills in apprehending the escapee. He is one of the foremost authorities in such apprehensions. He needs some help and asked for you."

"Sorry, gentlemen, I am in no mood to be part of a posse to capture people who break out of jail. Such men are dangerous and can hurt you," I said while trying not to get irritated that the train had stopped moving, which meant the trip would not end as soon as I had liked.

"No, no, it is not a man who escaped; it is a chimpanzee," said Mr. Smally. "It is a valuable one, I might add, and they want it returned safe and sound and they knew I was the person who might be able to do it. In fact, I am one of the few in the country that has developed the technique. Come now, we must move quickly while Quatro, (the name of his bulldog, I assumed,) can still pick up the scent."

Before any questions could be asked, Ronald and Mr. Smally rushed off the train, and my curiosity got the better of me so I followed. I wondered if the train would wait for us and, like he was reading my mind, Mr. Julian yelled that he had been instructed to stay put and not move until he either heard back from us or was told by the Portland office to move on.

We started walking up a steep hill away from the train, but before we went very far I asked the trio what it was that we were exactly expected to do, especially me since I seemed to have no part in the excursion. "Why I want you to record my, our, exploits in capturing the runaway chimp," said Mr. Smally.

Just as those words came out of his mouth Quatro and Ronald stopped dead in their tracks and pointed just east of the direction we were going. Mr. Smally looked in that direction also and gave us all a sign to lie on the ground. Quatro and Ronald immediately did so and I quickly followed.

I searched the area ahead of us but could not

see anything out of the ordinary. Just a bunch of tree branches filled with green leaves. Finally I noticed a furry looking animal sitting on a tree limb eating leaves. Then to my surprise I saw Mr. Smally crawling up the trunk of a tree behind and just a little lower than the one the chimp was on. He waved his hand which apparently was the signal for Ronald and Quatro to approach the bottom of the tree where the chimp was having lunch.

Ronald dropped Quatro's leash and the dog just sat there growling at the chimp. Ronald approached the base of the tree and with one end of the pole started poking the chimp who became very agitated. The chimp began jumping up and down, lost his balance and fell to the ground. As soon as the chimp landed, Quatro rushed up to him and chomped down on the chimp's testicles. The chimp let out a scream threw his arms in the air and at the same time Mr. Smally jumped from the adjacent tree and clamped the handcuffs around the chimp's wrists. After that Quatro let go, and the chimp curled up its legs; and Ronald quickly tied its legs together. The chimp was immobilized.

The pole was slipped thru the rope and handcuffs and Ronald and I carried the animal back to the train and put it in the baggage car for the short trip to the research center.

Over drinks that evening, I asked Mr. Smally

how he got into such a business and he said it was because when he was much younger he traveled with the circus as an acrobat and monkey keeper. He was about the same size as the monkeys so he got along with them well. Now and then they would escape from the traveling show and he would go after them. "What you just observed was a piece of art that took several attempts to master. I don't do it much any more, but as you can see I haven't lost my touch."

"You know I have been wondering about several things." I said. "I have it figured out why you carried the pole and the handcuffs and of course the rope, but why the shotgun?"

"Oh that is the easiest part of it all, if you stop and think about it," said a knowing Mr. Smally. "If by chance I happen to miscalculate my jump, which has happened at least three times, and I hit the ground before the chimp does, Ronald is instructed to shoot the dog."

15

Oh Donnie Boy

The rest of the trip did go uninterrupted. I finished compiling my notes and did an outline and was beginning to fill in the blanks. Before I could finish I was interrupted several times, none of which bothered me a bit. Some of the folks whom I had interviewed stopped by the observation deck to bid me a farewell. I made each one promise to drop me a line via email or snail mail to let me know what was happening in their lives. I had already asked the same of those passengers who were not going to the end the line. That is, I had asked everyone but Donnie.

As I was leaving the train I encountered Mr. Julian as he was getting back on to head east. He tipped his hat, smiled and said in a loud clear voice, "All aboard." I watched the Portland Express pull out of the Portland terminal, and I think I had perhaps a tear or two in one of my eyes. That is the problem with train rides. Just like Robert Lewis Stevenson wrote, "barely a glimpse and gone forever." I focused my eyes on the caboose and watched it fade from sight.

As I waved down a station porter to take my bags to the front of the terminal so I could catch a cab to catch a plane back home, I saw a young lady sitting across the tracks on a station bench, her hands folded in her lap, wearing an old fashioned gingham dress, and a suitcase sitting on the ground beside her.

She had a sad expression on her face and she slowly scanned those passengers who had disembarked, most of whom were heading towards the terminal exit like me.

I thought to myself, no, it could not be; what were the chances? Why not, I thought. I crossed the tracks and approached the young lady, "Ma'am, may I help you? You seem somewhat lost."

"That is very kind of you, sir, but I was supposed to meet someone here and as of yet he has not shown up. I guess I made a mistake. Things have been awfully confusing lately," the young girl said.

"Who were you supposed to meet, if I might ask?"

"My fiancée. We are supposed to get married. He is a sailor; name is Donnie, Donnie McGraw."

Why was I not surprised? "So you must be Lucy. Donnie talked about you a lot. He said you were going to meet him, but the place and circumstances kept changing. He got off in Ulysses."

"Don't tell me you are that guy who is doing some marketing research; well, I'll be. Is he ok? I mean is anything wrong? I guess we just got our wires crossed. Oh, I bet he did not get my last message. I told him that my mom had gotten better; the church paid for the operation, my boss at Butcher's found a replacement quicker than he thought and that I won $5000 in the Quick Pick Chicago Lottery. That's how I bought my ticket out here, replenished his bank account, and made a deposit on a nice little seaside condo just a few minutes from the base. Do you think they have another train leaving soon that will get me to Ulysses?

Feeling rather foolish about all the cynicism I wasted prejudging her, we tracked down the ticket master who had just closed his window for the night.

"Sorry folks, I know for certain that there is no train till next week that leaves here in that direction.

But do not despair, there is bus service that will take you there and it leaves in about an hour."

He gave us directions to the bus terminal and we hastily made tracks, no pun intended. As we reached the ticket window at the bus terminal, Lucy turned pale. "I forgot my purse with all my money." Without batting an eye I reached into my wallet and pulled out the University's travel credit card and purchased her the ticket.

I waved goodbye and started my slow walk back to the train station contemplating my dilemma. No cash, the University credit card was of the prepaid variety and I just reached its limit with my last purchase. How was I going to explain all this to Professor Simpson? It was then my Irish lucky charm found me and I came across Mr. Smally and Ronald with their gang of small relatives.

"Well, well, I thought you would have been heading back towards the Midwest by now," said Mr. Smally.

"Well, uh, well, I decided since I was out here I would take a short vacation. Never been to the northwest, nor have I ever seen the Pacific Ocean; don't know when I will have the opportunity again."

"Listen young man, I never did get around to telling you about all my adventures that may have a place in that report of yours. Since you've never been out this way why don't you travel with us to the coast and down to Hollywood where the reunion is to be held. I got a customized bus ready to pick us up in just a few minutes. What do you say? I will even make a call or two and make it so you won't have to take any vacation time. I know a guy who knows a guy. There won't be any problems for you at work." He saw me hesitate and he quickly added, "All expenses paid, even back to the University."

I really enjoyed my journey with my wee friends. The bus did get a little cramped now and then.

Epilogue

Mr. Smally was true to his words. He called a friend of his in the artificial equine insemination business whose daughter happened to be married to a marketing executive for one of the major motion picture studios in Hollywood. The executive made a pitch to the studio's president that there may be a story somewhere concerning Mr. Smally, the Portland Express, and the assignment I was given by the University. The studio president called Stanly Hoginfessor III, Portland Express President, who ran it through their marketing department where it was staffed around and found to have some merit and potential as a docudrama. The studio, having read my notes and first draft, said they would be interested in pursuing the matter further but only if I was allowed to be a script consultant. The Portland Executive guys called the University guys. All the guys met with Professor Simpson, the result being a nice few months' stay in sunny California. I might chronicle my time and adventures in California eventually. We shall see.

When the screen play was completed, there was little resemblance between what was and was not. I understood completely. I too, now and then, use the Hollywood model called verisimilitude, loosely defined as never letting facts interfere with a good story.

I am not sure when the film will go into production or when it will be released. I will let you know.

About the Author

Photo by Brian McAnally

Conley Stone "Snapper" McAnally is a retired U.S. Army Reserve officer and public school teacher. He is a former columnist for *The Examiner* of Independence, Missouri, where he cataloged his experience as a teacher in "bush" Alaska among the Yupik and Inupaque Eskimos. Several of his observations have been published in *Whispering Wind*, a magazine about Native American life and culture. His blog, The Adventures of Conley McAnally, is at conleymcanally.blogspot.com. He is also the the author of several short stories and novellas. He is the father of five children and grandfather of 15. He currently resides with his wife Beverly in Tucson, Arizona.

ENTER THE WEIRD WORLD OF
COLIN LEE CAMPBELL

FUNERAL TRAIN AND OTHER STORIES

The first book by Colin Lee Campbell is now available on Amazon, with a handsome new cover and bonus story. The ten tales collected here run the gamut from the fantastic to the macabre.

TALES FROM CAPE CITY

In nine action-packed, darkly comedic tales, Colin Campbell takes us on a whirlwind tour of Cape City's past and present, seen through the eyes of heroes and villains who redefine what it means to be "super."

PHARAOH PUBLISHING

"TALES TIME FORGOT"

Classic Pulp Novels Return to Print!

FROM THE CREATOR OF NERO WOLFE

Rex Stout, the creator of master sleuth Nero Wolfe, cut his teeth writing adventure stories for pulp magazines. This early example of his work is rife with fist-fights, escapes, beautiful women, degenerate natives, and underground explorations, as two brothers and a femme fatale find themselves trapped in an undiscovered netherworld of darkness, danger and desire.

FROM THE CREATOR OF TARZAN AND JOHN CARTER

Edgar Rice Burroughs, master of the pulp art, tries his hand at a *Prisoner of Zenda*-like tale. Barney, a rural man from Nebraska, is unaware that he shares the blood of kings. In the fictional European nation of Lutha, young Barney finds himself mistaken for the rightful king Leopold. The true king has been imprisoned by his wicked uncle. No man's pawn, Barney makes himself master of the situation.

THE CLASSIC TALE OF HIGH ADVENTURE RETURNS

England, 1757...Moonfleet. A village with a secret. An orphan lad with a dream. A band of wily smugglers. A legend of lost treasure. J. Meade Falkner blends these ingredients into a model tale of swashbuckling adventure in the style of Robert Louis Stevenson and early Talbot Mundy.

PHARAOH PUBLISHING

THE MOST IMPORTANT BOOK EVER WRITTEN

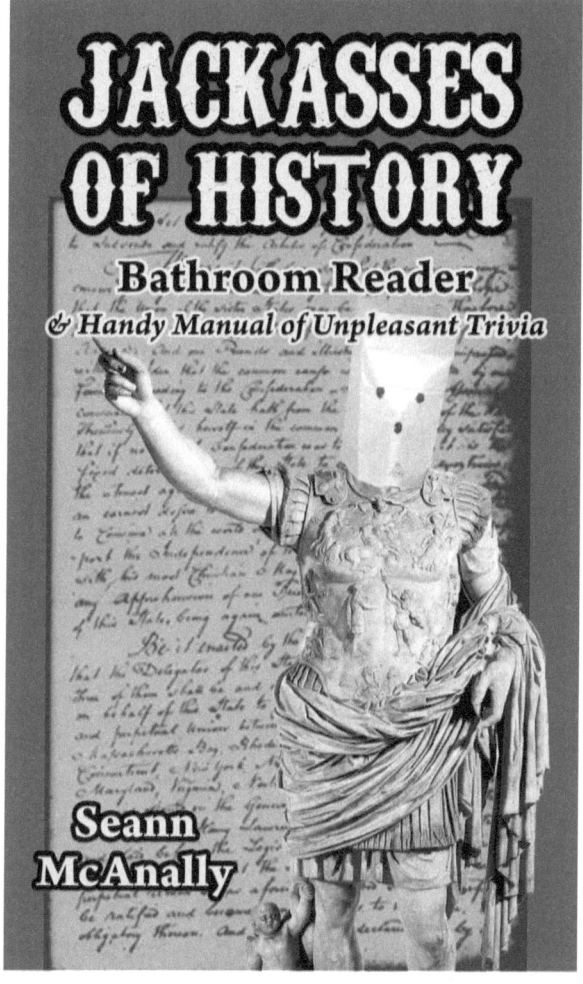

Actually, it's not. Norman Baker said that about his autobiography.
Why? He was a jackass. In this book you'll meet 20 losers, killers, fools
and criminals—the Jackasses of History!

AVAILABLE NOW ON AMAZON AND AT
WWW.PHARAOHPUBLISHINGUSA.COM

Pharaoh Publishing USA is an indepdendent publisher
of books, music and games in the Heart of America.

We do not accept unsolicited materials.

Contact us at pharaohpublishingusa@gmail.com.